Two Hands to Hold

By
Anita Castro

Illustrated by
Dean Wroth

Jason and Nordic Publishers, Inc.
Hollidaysburg, Pennsylvania

Library of Congress Cataloging-in-Publication Data

Castro, Anita.
   Two hands to hold / by Anita Castro ; illustrated by Dean Wroth.
      pages cm. -- (Turtle books)
   Summary: "Addie is a little girl who is facing serious medical issues.
With the loving support of her family, teacher and friends, she faces
the future with love and a positive attitude"-- Provided by publisher.
   ISBN 978-0-944727-58-4 (library binding : alk. paper) -- ISBN
978-0-944727-57-7 (perfect bound paper : alk. paper)
   [1. Sick--Fiction.] I. Wroth, Dean, illustrator. II. Title.
   PZ7.C2687454Tw 2013
   [E]--dc23
                                              2012033833

Printed in the United States of America
On acid free paper

ISBN 978-0-944727-58-4 Library binding
ISBN 978-0-944727-57-7 perfect bound paper

To Sam, Laura, and all my family,
thank you for believing in me
more than I ever did myself, *and*

To Krista, whose skill and kindness
has smoothed the hardest of roads
for so many families.

My best day was when we all went to the zoo together, Mommy and Daddy and my little brother, Sammy and me.

Daddy bought balloons for my brother and me.

We looked at all the animals. I liked the
monkeys best. I saw the Mommy Monkey
holding her baby's hand. All day Mommy held
my hand.

My scariest day was the day the doctor
said, "Addie has to go to the hospital for tests."
I wasn't too scared because Mommy was
holding my hand.

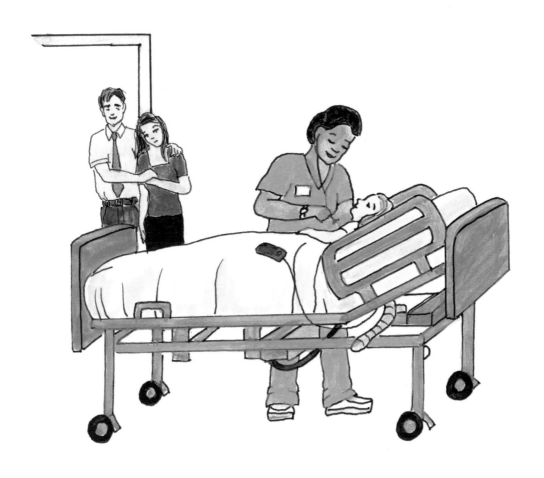

At the hospital a nurse put me in a bed that went up and down. She listened to my heart.

I could tell that Mommy and Daddy were very sad.

I asked if I'd done something wrong, but Mommy gave me a big hug and said, "No, you are a very good girl and we love you SO MUCH!"

I know it was true, because she was holding my hand.

The nurse took some blood for tests and the next day I had an x-ray.

I asked if I was going to die, and Mommy said, "I don't know, but whatever happens, I'll be right here holding your hand!"

I asked Mommy if I was sick because I pinched my brother and took his candy.

She laughed and said, "No, but today you are going home so you had better stop pinching your brother!"

I know she wasn't mad, because she was holding my hand.

Some days I don't feel good so I stay in bed.
I soon feel better because Mommy sits with me
and holds my hand.

Other days when I don't feel good, Mommy
reads me my favorite books.

When I'm scared I talk to Mommy. She tells me that she'll make sure I'm always comfortable, and that I'll always be part of our family. She says she has two hands so that one hand can always be holding on to me.

Yesterday I felt much better and we went to the zoo again.

Daddy pushed my chair fast and made race car noises. Sammy and Mommy ran alongside, laughing with me.

Daddy bought us balloons again.
Then we saw more animals.

When we looked at the crocodiles, I was glad Mommy was holding my hand. He looked like he was smiling at Sammy and me. He had a very scary smile.

The funniest part was when the elephant sprayed us with water from his trunk. Sammy ran and hid behind Daddy, but I just laughed.

There are lots of things I don't like about being sick, like staying in bed a lot and getting treatments at the hospital, but there are some things I like about it.

I like that Mommy and Daddy spend a lot of time with me and my brother.

I like that I get to eat more ice cream, and
that sometimes I get presents like my new
princess crown.

Sometimes I have to stay in bed and Mommy plays games with me.

She hangs a blanket over the bed posts like a tent and we play that we're camping.

Sammy likes to play that, too. But he gets silly. Then Sammy and the tent fall on the floor in a pile.

I like to play with Mommy making hand
shadows on the wall.

When I get tired, I take a nap while Mommy holds my hand.

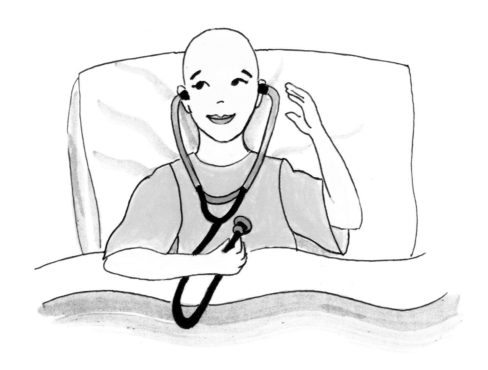

When the nurse comes for a visit, she listens to my heart. Sometimes she lets me listen, too. My heart sounds like, "...ba BUMP, ba BUMP!"

Have you ever listened to your heart?

One day the kids at school made cards and wrote notes to bring to me at home.

For fun, Mommy made me a cat pajama
suit. She made my nose red and drew whiskers
on my cheeks.

The teacher and some of my friends brought the cards and notes to me. They all wore animal pajamas, too.

There are lots of things I don't like about being sick, but there is one thing that I do like most of all.

I have lots of friends and I know Mommy will always be here, holding my hand.